To my nieces and nephews,
Sakura, Miles, Kotaro, Taylor, and Yamato-
May you always have the courage
To follow your heart

Can you hear them?
Listen closely.
Close your eyes.

Listen

Words by: Tatsuya Fushimi
Pictures by: Britney Vu

ISBN: 9781737680925

Cover design and illustrations by Britney Vu.

Not the radio,
The TV,
Or the cars driving by.

They've been with you
From the very start.

The voices in your mind
And in your heart.

But understand they're different.
Know it very clear.

They can kill your dreams
Or help you persevere.

In your mind
Are two voices up there.

One is positive, the other negative.
The negative voice NEVER plays fair.

Your mind says, "ANYTHING is possible!"
Reminds you how gifted you are.

Or it holds you back, beats you down,
And makes sure you don’t go far.

It shouts,

"Dream BIG!"

"Keep GOING!"

"You're amazing!"

"You're free!"

Or tells you, “You're stupid.”
“You’re not good enough.”
“You’re weak.”
And of course, “You’re ugly.”

One day it says, “You’re loved!”
“You’re rich!”
“Everything will be fine!”

The next day, “You’re poor.”
“Just give up.”
“You don't have enough time.”

The voices in your mind
Will try to trick you every day.

They'll affect your feelings
To forget what your heart truly wants to say.

Do you compare yourself to people?
Do you care too much about what they say?

These are the two biggest ways
These voices lead you astray.

So next time you hear people speak
Notice the words they say.

Some are positive, most are negative.
They, too, hear voices that get in their way.

But here's the important thing.
Understand that YOU have the choice.

YOU have the power.
To listen to either voice.

Now, in your heart
There's only one voice.
This one must never be ignored.

Some people call it intuition.
Others say gut feeling.
It's your superpower forevermore.

It’s a feeling deep inside.
Your guiding light.

It’s always on.
It's always right.

It's very wise.
Knows what's best for you.
It never lies.

It's fearless.
Pulls you forward
Even if you don't know why.

The voice in your heart
Is pure love.
Something only YOU can hear.

Some people will never understand.
It may be hard to explain.
But you mustn't fear.

Trust the voice in your heart
Even if you feel alone.

This is key to your greatness
That the world must be shown.

Your heart knows where to go.
It'll show you the way.

Just take a step in that direction.
Choose to be bold every day!

At first, your mind may be scared
Because of the unknown.

Be patient, it will follow.
And expand your comfort zone.

Have the courage
To let your heart lead.
Take care of this powerful voice.

Does the world see the REAL you?
It's your responsibility,
Your choice.

Dance your heart out
Trust the process + keep practicing

About the Author

Tatsuya Fushimi is passionate about self-development and is a seeker of his truth. A life coach and entrepreneur, he is inspired to simplify his perspectives gained in adulthood through children's books. His desire is to empower others with more clarity and awareness to help them reach their highest potential. A Southern California native, he enjoys playing golf and engaging in deep conversations about life with everyone he meets.

Instagram: @tatsuyafushimi

About the Illustrator

Britney (Bri) Vu is an artist and illustrator. Her love for art came from listening to her mom and grandmother read to her every day. She was fascinated with the images that helped tell those stories, appreciating every detail on each page and then running off to draw and paint pictures of her own. As she grew up, curiosity has invited her to explore many passions. Still, her heart always calls her back to make art to create joy, magic and connection with others. Born and raised in the San Francisco Bay Area, she enjoys hikes by the ocean & snuggling with her three cats - Sid, Shadow and Stanley.

Instagram: @britneyvu_

CPSIA information can be obtained
at www.ICGtesting.com
Printed in the USA
LVHW071624301021
701975LV00006B/185

9 781737 680925